Beneath the
Hill Country Sky

A Texas Mystery of
Secrets and Shadows

"This book is a work of fiction. While the character and their journey were inspired by the spirit and creativity of a real individuals, the story, characters, and events contained within are entirely products of imagination and are not based on real life. This narrative was created with the assistance of artificial intelligence."

By Richard Dell Schwarz

Foreword

There are places in this world where silence lingers longer than sound, where history is not written in books but whispered between cedar trees and buried in the stone foundations of forgotten buildings. *Beneath the Hill Country Sky* was born from such a place.

This story is not just about a missing girl or a troubled stranger. It is about community—what it hides, what it protects, and what it sometimes refuses to face. Set in the rugged heart of 1880s Texas, in a town both fictional and familiar, this novel explores the fragile line between justice and peace, and the cost of crossing it.

I wrote this book out of a love for the land and the people who forged lives in its harsh beauty. The Texas Hill Country has long held stories worth telling—some bright with hope, others shadowed with sorrow. This one is both.

At its center is Klaus Richter, a man shaped by grief and guided by conscience, whose search for redemption challenges the very soil he hoped would bury his past. Through him, and through the voices of those he meets along the way, I hope to give readers not just a mystery to solve, but a history to feel.

Thank you for stepping into Sisterdale. May its secrets move you, and its truth linger long after the final page.

— Richard Schwarz
Boerne, Texas

Table of contents

Contents

Chapter 1: The New World's Promise

The steamship Hansa lurched against the pier at Galveston on a blistering July afternoon in 1883, her whistle shrieking like a wounded gull. Klaus Richter stood midway down the gangplank, steadying the small boy in front of him with one hand while the other clenched a worn leather satchel. The boy—an Irish lad he did not know—bolted ahead the instant his boots touched the boards, and Klaus finally exhaled. After nineteen days of cramped quarters, spoiled stores, and the constant groan of the Atlantic, the pier felt miraculously solid. The smell surprised him most: not just salt and tar, as he had imagined, but coffee roasting somewhere inland, orange peels, hot horseflesh, and a faint medicinal odor that reminded him of a chemist's shop in Hamburg.

He forced himself to take it all in slowly, as his mother had once told him: *Beschreibe mit den Augen, Junge—describe with your eyes before you do with your tongue.* A lumber crane swung overhead, dripping seawater. Stevedores in straw hats shouted in English and Spanish, while a group of colored women balanced wicker baskets of oysters on their heads and sang a hymn in four-part harmony. To the south, the Gulf shone white, so bright that it stung his eyes. Somewhere out of sight a brass band battered through a lively polka, out of tune yet exultant.

Klaus let the orchestra of the port wash over him until his heart slowed. Then he lifted the satchel's strap across his chest and stepped forward into America.

He was twenty-eight, of middling height, with the lean strength of a craftsman who has spent half his life coaxing obedience from stubborn oak. A charcoal-gray linen coat, patched at the elbows, hung loose on his wiry frame. His hair—dark, thick, and sensibly trimmed at the nape—was damp with sweat, but his piercing blue eyes remained clear, watchful. A stranger reading those eyes might guess him to be cautious by nature. Few would guess the shadow hooked behind that caution, the reason he had sold the family shop in Braunschweig, kissed his sister good-bye, and boarded the Hansa two steps ahead of rumors that threatened to become something uglier than talk.

Texas, he had concluded, was far enough to make the world forget him, and perhaps far enough that he might forget himself.

The emigration-clerk's office occupied a scorched tin shed perched between two cotton warehouses. Inside, perspiring officials inked the newcomers' names into ledgers thick as bibles. A green-eyed woman with a ledger labeled K–R gestured Klaus forward.

"Name."

"Richter, Klaus."

"Trade?"

"Tischler—carpenter," he said, then corrected himself: "Cabinetmaker."

The woman's pen scratched. "Funds on hand?"

He placed the little drawstring pouch on the table—fifty-four dollars, mostly Prussian silver exchanged in New Orleans. The woman weighed it by feel, recorded a figure, and slid it back without counting; a line of steaming passengers pressed behind him, and precision was a casualty of heat.

"Final destination?"

"Sisterdale," he said carefully, employing the rolling *r* he had practiced.

The woman frowned. "Never heard of her. County?"

He unfolded a letter—yellowed, rain-stained—
addressed from *Johann Braun, Land-Agent, Sisterdale,
Kendall Cty, Tex.*, and laid it before her.

"Kendall," she muttered, copying the word. "Very
well, Mr. Richter. Next!"

Outside, some passengers kissed the ground in
gratitude. Klaus did not. He had no appetite for
spectacle. Instead he found a boardinghouse—the
Schreiber Haus, run by a Lutheran widow from
Frankfurt—and rented a cot in the attic for two
nights while he searched for transport inland. The
mattress reeked of turpentine, but at least the
woman spoke his language, and the bitter chicory
coffee she served at dawn tasted like possibility.

Klaus signed onto a freight caravan bound for San
Antonio: seven wagons, two drovers on each, plus a
stagecoach carrying a Chicago businessman who
fretted incessantly about bandits. They departed at
sunrise the third day. Galveston's clapboard houses
gave way to muddy prairie studded with dwarf
palmetto and sunflowers tall as men. The road was
rutted, its puddles breeding swarms of mosquitoes
whose whine merged with the endless creak of
wagon beds.

The traveling company proved a study in frontier
diversity. Beside Klaus on the lead wagon sat Tomás

Aguilar, a Tejano muleteer whose broad-brimmed hat shaded a grin like a split melon. Tomás possessed a gift for story—how the Comanche once rode through this grass tall enough to hide a horse, how Sam Houston had slept beneath a pecan tree outside Gonzales, how the railroad would soon link San Antonio to the coast and make mule freighters obsolete.

Klaus listened more than he spoke, absorbing the rhythm of English as if carving a groove for it in his mind. When Tomás asked about Germany, Klaus spoke generally of snow-blanketed winters and black-forest pines, but he never mentioned courtrooms or the Kaiser's constabulary, never spoke the girl's name whose fate had sealed his own. Some losses, he believed, became heavier each time they were lifted into words.

The prairie gradually folded into hills. Live oaks replaced palmetto, their limbs twisted as if caught in permanent wind. Deer trailed the caravan at dusk, nibbling the tender shoots that wagon wheels exposed. One evening a thunderstorm galloped in from the north; lightning stitched the horizon while the drovers huddled under tarpaulins singing bawdy ballads in three languages. Klaus lay awake counting the seconds between flash and boom, recalling how as a boy he had measured distance by sound: *three seconds equals a kilometer.* Across an ocean, the equation held true. He found comfort in that.

San Antonio welcomed them with adobe walls, crooked streets, and the ringing of mission bells calling the faithful to vespers. The Alamo's limestone façade glowed pink in the sunset. Yet the city churned with commerce—cotton factors, saloons, blacksmith forges hammering late into night—too crowded for a man who wanted his footprints swallowed by grass. Klaus camped one night behind a stable, then purchased a seat on a freighter's buckboard headed to Fredericksburg and points beyond.

The driver, old Herr Dietz, was Swabian by birth and delighted to discover a passenger who could discuss Goethe while spitting tobacco juice with frontier efficiency. Dietz explained that German immigrants had seeded a constellation of hamlets across the Hill Country—Fredericksburg, Boerne, Comfort, Sisterdale—each small enough to count its souls without pen and paper. Sisterdale, he said, sat in a bend of the Guadalupe River, famous for peaches, limestone, and a single banyan tree imported from India that inexplicably thrived beside the church.

"Why there?" Dietz asked as cicadas droned.

Klaus considered. "Because it is small enough that my name means nothing."

Dietz chewed on that thought, then spat. "Names have a way of gathering weight, *Freund*. Even among fewer mouths."

They reached Fredericksburg at noon, tethered the horses behind a beer garden, and Dietz introduced Klaus to Johann Braun, the land-agent. Braun, a barrel-chested Bavarian in a lavender waistcoat, welcomed Klaus as if greeting a cousin. Over plates of venison sausage he produced a map earned from the General Land Office—its edges browned, folds splitting—and jabbed a stubby finger at a square three miles west of Sisterdale labeled *Lot 42, 17 acres, cedar & creek frontage.*

"Fifty dollars for the deed, six percent interest if paid over two years," Braun said. "There is a cabin, but the roof is sorry. You are a carpenter—put your hammer to it and she'll serve."

Klaus counted his coins, hesitated, then signed. He felt the odd exhilaration of a man gambling everything on one throw because he no longer owns anything else worth wagering.

Braun arranged a wagon the following dawn. The final road—really a goat track—wound between craggy limestone bluffs tufted with Ashe juniper. Prickly pear, their red fruit splitting under the sun, flanked the trail. Klaus glimpsed wild turkey flushing from the underbrush and, once, the silver flash of a spring that burbled from a cliff and vanished into reeds.

Then Sisterdale unfolded beneath them.

The settlement occupied a shallow bowl of meadow, its dozen stone houses crouched like pale sentinels along a green ribbon of water. A church steeple, modest yet elegant, speared the sky. Peach orchards traced the slopes, their leaves glossy in the late-afternoon glare. Smoke curled lazily from chimneys. Dietz clicked his tongue. "There she is. Quiet as a sleeping cat—until you step on her tail."

They rattled across a low wooden bridge. Children fishing beneath it waved. Dogs barked and then, recognizing neither man nor wagon, fell silent in a collective canine frown. Dietz halted before a whitewashed store whose sign read Schmidt & Co. General Mercantile: Dry Goods, Hardware, Patent Medicines.

Klaus thanked the old driver, shouldered his satchel, and stepped onto the packed-dirt street that would, for better or worse, be his horizon.

Sisterdale's Embrace, and Wariness

The townsfolk studied him with undisguised interest. Not suspicion—at least not yet—but a keen curiosity born of isolation. He answered their nods politely, his German accent drawing smiles of recognition. Several spoke the Swabian dialect; others had adopted English verbs grafted onto German grammar like mismatched dowels.

Klaus located his property at the edge of town: seventeen acres hemmed by cedar breaks, with a shack listing westward as if drunk on its own neglect. The door hung from one hinge; the sod roof sprouted bluebonnet in defiance of gravity. Yet water from the nearby spring tasted cold and lime-sweet, and a pair of live oaks shaded the cabin's southern face. He unpacked, unrolled a pallet, and slept eleven hours straight.

Morning found him repairing the door, singing *"Die Gedanken sind frei"* under his breath. By noon he had replaced warped floorboards, chinked gaps with river clay, and discovered a nest of scorpions in the hearth, which he removed with less grace than speed. Blisters stippled his palms, but the ache was honest. The past year his hands had known only the anxiety of courtroom benches and clandestine train rides. Work felt medicinal.

Word circulated fast. By sundown a lanky farmer named Ernst Schneider arrived offering a crock of stew and a request: could the newcomer spare two days to rebuild a chicken coop flattened in last month's storm? Klaus agreed. Work meant money; money meant nails, lamp oil, seeds.

The next weeks blurred into labor. He mended the bell tower at St. Peter's, planed cedar for porch railings, and fashioned a cradle for a couple whose first child was overdue. Each project paid coins or produce, but greater than payment was the slow weaving of his name into village conversation: *Herr Richter, the quiet carpenter.*

Yet beneath that weave, a tighter pattern emerged— subtle, but unmistakable to a mind attuned to silences. Conversations sometimes knotted when he approached: Frau Lang stopped mid-sentence, cheeks flushing; Pastor Voltz changed subjects with a cough that sounded rehearsed. In the mercantile one afternoon he heard a young storekeeper joke that Sisterdale did not lock its doors at night "unless the hills start whispering." When he asked what that meant, the youth swallowed and pretended not to understand.

Klaus told himself it was immigrant superstition. Still, the question lodged like a splinter.

The Schmidt Family

The Schmidts were Sisterdale's unofficial royalty. Their limestone house, three gables and a widow's walk, sat on a rise overlooking the peach orchards. Herr Schmidt—Friedrich by baptism, Fritz by common usage—stood well over six feet, with shoulders forged by decades behind a plow that he had since traded for ledgers and tenants. His beard, streaked silver, framed a mouth quick to smile yet quicker to flatten when challenged.

Frau Helene Schmidt seldom ventured beyond her parlor, but her influence radiated like candlelight through lace windows: a subscription to a New York fashion magazine, a pianoforte shipped from Stuttgart, rose bushes coaxed into improbable bloom by imported fertilizer. Their one child, Anna, seventeen that spring, carried her mother's refinement and her father's vitality in disarming measure. She rode astride, scandalizing older matrons, and quoted Schiller with unabashed zeal. The valley adored her.

Klaus first glimpsed Anna at the river ford, where schoolchildren splashed barefoot after Sunday lessons. She guided her sorrel pony through the shallows, skirts hitched, laughing as water spattered her cheeks. Their eyes met briefly. Hers were hazel, flecked with green like lichen on stone. She gave a nod that seemed to say, *I see you, stranger,* then turned to chase a younger boy threatening to dive from a boulder.

The exchange lasted seconds, yet the warmth of it lingered through the evening while Klaus whittled a spoon by lamplight. He told himself she was merely friendly, that the tilt of her head meant nothing. But in truth he had not felt so recognized since leaving Germany, and the recognition stirred a hope he had studiously buried.

July Harvest Dance

July's closing Saturday brought the harvest dance, held in the barn of a Czech dairyman whose accordion skills compensated for uneven floorboards. Lanterns dangled from rafters, haloing dust motes like startled fireflies. Women in calico twirled; men slapped boots in polka rhythm. Klaus, leaning against a support beam, sipped watered beer and rehearsed excuses not to dance.

Anna Schmidt cut through the throng, dress the
color of new wheat. She extended a hand.
"Herr Richter, will you stand there all night guarding
the wall?"

He stammered, betrayed by rusty English. But she
grinned and tugged. The accordion launched into
"Ach, du lieber Augustin," and Klaus found himself
airborne in laughter. His feet remembered waltz
steps taught by an aunt in Braunschweig, and the
barn blurred around them in concentric rings of
music, lantern-light, and hay-scent.

Afterward, breathless, they walked outside where
grasshoppers rasped. Anna spoke of her plans: she
would travel to Austin in autumn to study at a
women's academy, learn shorthand, perhaps publish
essays on botany. Sisterdale, she said, was lovely but
small—*"ein Käfig mit goldenen Stäben*—a cage with
gilded bars." Klaus nodded, understanding more
than she guessed.

Yet behind her enthusiasm he detected tension: a
glance over her shoulder toward the barn, an abrupt
silence when footsteps crunched nearby. When
Herr Schmidt emerged calling her name, she
squeezed Klaus's arm once, as if pledging trust,
before hurrying back. Her father's arm encircled her
shoulders in a gesture that looked comforting but

clasped too tightly. Klaus watched until lanterns were doused and the night swallowed the valley.

Flashbacks: Germany

Certain nights the Hill Country air cooled enough that embers from Klaus's hearth glowed blue. He would sit at the small pine table, journal open, pen idle. From the satchel he removed a photograph: a young woman named Clara Drechsler, hair pinned with mother-of-pearl combs, eyes merry beneath the photographer's magnesium flash. They had promised marriage the winter after her apprentice contract ended.

Then the mill-owner's son decided he wanted Clara for himself. A fabricated accusation—petty theft—sullied her reputation. Klaus testified on her behalf; the court dismissed him as a tradesman of no consequence. Clara, humiliated and unemployable, drowned herself in the Oker River the following spring. When Klaus confronted the mill-owner's son with a carpenter's mallet raised in trembling hands, police arrived before blows fell. He spent six nights in a cell, released only when his father sold half their stock of walnut lumber for bail. The magistrate advised him to "consider emigration if he desired a clean slate." Two months later the family workshop stood empty and the Hansa's manifest bore his name.

Each time those memories surfaced, Klaus folded them back into the photograph and returned it to the satchel, as if resealing a wound. But wounds breathe; they remember. He feared what would happen if Sisterdale reopened his.

The Day Silence Fell

Summer thickened. Locusts sang. Klaus reroofed the church, its cedar shakes shimmering like fish scales. On August 14 he walked to the mercantile for turpentine. The usual porch chatter had evaporated; two men stood rigid, coffee cups forgotten in their hands. Inside, Frau Schmidt, the proprietor, paced behind the counter, face drained of color. She glanced at Klaus as if through him.

"Was ist los?" he whispered. What's wrong?

She opened her mouth, closed it, and pointed to the notice board near the door. A sheet of paper, edges trembling in the breeze, read:

Missing—Anna Schmidt
Last seen: Morning of August 13, riding chestnut mare *Freia* toward Guadalupe Creek.

Any information please inform Sheriff J. Stone. Reward offered.

Klaus stared until the words blurred. Behind him a child sobbed. He looked to Frau Schmidt again, but she turned away, shoulders shaking.

That evening torches bobbed through the orchards as search parties plowed between peach rows. Klaus joined the eastern group. They scoured creek beds, called her name, listened for hoofbeats. Owls answered. Nothing more.

At dawn the sheriff arrived from Comfort— Jeb Stone, burly, moustache drooping like melted wax. He questioned Fritz Schmidt briefly in the parlor, emerged wiping sweat, and addressed the assembled townsfolk.

"My deputies and I find no sign of foul play," he declared. "Miss Schmidt likely rode off of her own accord, maybe toward San Antonio. Young folks get restless."

Murmurs rippled—disbelief, but also relief, as if an official statement allowed dread to be shelved. Sheriff Stone outlined no organized search beyond voluntary efforts. Klaus noted how quickly certain men accepted the verdict. One even patted

Fritz Schmidt's arm, promising prayers rather than action.

Klaus imagined Clara's name on a similar notice back home, how swiftly authorities had labeled her despair an unfortunate *Frauenhysterie* and moved on. Looking now at the orchard, he tasted that same arrogance, sour as spoiled cider.

First Clue

Two days later Klaus repaired a cattle gate on the Schmidt property. Mid-afternoon he rested in the shade of a live oak, scanning the terrain. A glint caught his eye near a clump of switchgrass where hoofprints veered. Kneeling, he uncovered a small brooch—silver filigree shaped like edelweiss, its clasp bent. He had seen it pinned to Anna's bodice at the harvest dance.

Carefully he slid the brooch into a kerchief, then studied the ground. The soil showed gouges where a horse had skidded. Nearby, cedar branches snapped at odd angles suggested something—or someone— had forced passage off the trail. Yet the official search had reportedly ended at the ford, a quarter-mile away.

Klaus returned the brooch to his pocket. He should deliver it to Sheriff Stone, he thought. But Stone had already written Anna off. Instead Klaus walked to the river alone, searching downstream for additional trace—boot heel, ribbon, hoofprint—but dusk swallowed the clues. Water gurgled, indifferent.

He spent that night pacing his cabin. Each tick of his pocket watch reminded him that delay smothered opportunity. But he also knew small towns could resent meddling, especially from an outsider. He considered confiding in Pastor Voltz, but Voltz, though kind, worshipped consensus and might counsel patience. Klaus recalled Tomás Aguilar's words on the trail: *Names gather weight.* He felt his name acquiring weight already, pulled by the brooch in his pocket like a lodestone.

Cabin Visitors

A week after the disappearance, a knock startled Klaus at near-midnight. He opened the door to find Helene Schmidt and Frau Lang, the midwife, both cloaked. Helene's eyes were red, voice ragged.

"We heard you found something of Anna's," she whispered. Word traveled on gusts in Sisterdale. Klaus fetched the kerchief, unwrapped the brooch.

Helene pressed it to her lips, stifling a sob.
Frau Lang frowned. "Where exactly did you find it?"

Klaus described the location. Lang exchanged a glance with Helene—some silent conversation heavy with implication. Then the midwife thanked him stiffly and shepherded Helene outside. Klaus watched them merge with shadows beyond the porch. Their visit brought him neither clarity nor comfort, only the sense that he had stepped onto a narrowing path.

Anonymous Warning

Two days later his mallet broke clean at the handle while he repaired the schoolhouse door. The break puzzled him—a fresh hickory handle should not snap under modest force. Examining the fracture, he discovered a fine saw-cut hidden beneath surface varnish, designed to fail.

That evening, returning from the well, he noticed boot tracks circling his cabin—heavy, hobnailed, unfamiliar. On the threshold lay a single cedar branch stripped of bark. He had seen similar branches tied to fence posts in Prussia as warnings: *Leave.*

Klaus tasted iron at the back of his throat. He had fled three thousand leagues to escape one injustice; Sisterdale beckoned him toward another. Clara's face flickered behind his eyelids. He banked the cabin fire, sat at the table, and wrote a name he had vowed to forget: *Clara Drechsler*—a witness, he told himself, to whatever promise he was about to make.

I will not turn away this time.

Closing Scene of Chapter

Before dawn he walked to the old grist mill that squatted beside the Guadalupe like a mausoleum. Locals said it had burned during the war, though no one detailed whose torches set it alight. Klaus stepped through a gap in the charred doorway, lantern raised. Dust motes swirled in the beam, and the air smelled of mold and riverweed.

He spotted chalk marks on a stone pillar—initials A.S. intertwined with a crude heart. Beneath, fresher scratches gouged the stone as though a blade had struck in anger. A length of ribbon—navy, patterned with tiny white asters—lay half-buried in silt. He pocketed it.

From somewhere above, a board creaked. Klaus froze, extinguished the lantern, and pressed against the wall. A silhouette crossed the ruined loft, then vanished. When he relit the lantern the loft was empty save for fluttering bats.

Outside, dawn bled violet across the hills. Klaus stood on the riverbank, pulse hammering, as turkey vultures wheeled overhead in lazy spirals. The water streamed past, unhurried, reflecting nothing of the secrets it carried.

He realized Sisterdale was no refuge; it was a crucible. The peace he had sought would demand a price measured not in dollars but in courage. Somewhere among these cedar hills lay the answer to a girl's disappearance and perhaps the redemption of a carpenter haunted by another girl drowned far away.

Klaus turned toward the village. Lanterns flickered awake in kitchen windows as families rose for chores, unaware that the quiet newcomer was about to tug a thread gripping the whole fabric of their valley. He squared his shoulders, adjusted the satchel where brooch and ribbon now rested together, and walked into the pale light of a Texas dawn, resolved that neither silence nor threats would keep him from following where the thread led.

Chapter 2 - Whispers in the Wind.

The morning after Anna Schmidt's disappearance, Sisterdale awoke not with screams or sirens, but with an almost defiant quiet. Birds still called from the pecan trees. Smoke still rose in thin blue ribbons from chimneys. But a hush had settled beneath those ordinary sounds—an uneasy stillness that did not belong in a valley so fond of song.

Klaus Richter noticed it first at the well. Normally, the morning line of women and children would chatter while they waited for the pulley bucket to make its slow descent and rise. But this time, when he approached with his water tin, the talk died like a wind snuffed out. A few murmured greetings were offered—thin, brittle—but none lingered to chat. One girl dropped her pail in such a hurry she forgot to retrieve it.

Klaus bent to pick it up, noting the faint tremble in her hands as she thanked him and scurried away.

The town had not forgotten Anna. Quite the opposite—they were remembering her with every breath not spoken.

He resumed his work, repairing a fencepost on the Lang property that morning and helping Ernst Schneider align a warped window frame in the afternoon. From a distance, Sisterdale seemed to carry on as usual. Klaus hammered, sawed, and swept, the rhythm of work steady and familiar. But people glanced over their shoulders more now. Conversations drifted into vagueness when he passed. When he asked a direct question—"Did you hear anything the night Anna disappeared?" or "Had she quarreled with her father recently?"—he was met with averted gazes or the tired refrain, "Sheriff Stone is handling it."

Was he?

He hadn't seen Stone since the sheriff made his dismissive remarks and rode off toward Comfort. No formal posse had been assembled. No fresh flyers posted. Sisterdale seemed to be willing the event away, as if silence could erase the absence.

Klaus's instincts, sharpened long ago by grief and injustice, stirred uncomfortably.

Despite the town's strange quiet, Klaus continued to find work. His reputation as a skilled carpenter had grown, and his manner—reserved, respectful, focused—made him an easy man to trust with a roof or a barn door. He took little pay, asking only what was fair, and never bartered for gossip.

At least, not openly.

He had learned in Germany that towns protected themselves with half-truths as much as with fences. If Sisterdale meant to close its ranks, he would observe until it cracked.

Each evening, he sat on his rebuilt porch with a small cup of coffee, watching the town's rhythms. Schoolchildren walked home in threes and fours. A man might stop to tip his hat; a woman might glance curiously from behind her lace curtains. Yet the routine never felt quite right after the search ended. It was as if a page had been torn from the village calendar, and no one dared replace it.

On Wednesdays, Klaus made his way to the general store—Schmidt & Co.—to buy nails, flour, or oil. The store had become his primary window into Sisterdale's unspoken truths.

It was here he first met Liesl.

Liesl was sixteen, lean and sharp-eyed, with dark hair she wore in a thick braid tied with a red ribbon. Her sleeves were often rolled to her elbows as she tallied crates or organized the ledger with ink-stained fingers. Though she addressed customers with the customary "yes, sir" or "no, ma'am," she spoke with a clarity and speed that betrayed a bright mind kept busy by more than shelf-stock.

When Klaus first asked her about rope prices, she replied without looking up, "Five cents a yard, but if you're planning to hang yourself over town gossip, I wouldn't waste good twine."

He blinked. "Pardon?"

She looked up, a wry smile tugging at her lips. "Just guessing. You've been asking questions."

Klaus offered a quiet smile in return. "And you've been listening."

She leaned on the counter. "That's what we do here. Listen. Store walls have better ears than the church."

He tilted his head. "And do those ears tell you anything about Anna?"

Liesl hesitated. Then she glanced toward the back room before answering. "Not unless you want your business to vanish overnight."

Klaus nodded slowly. "You think I should stop?"

She shrugged. "I think Anna wouldn't have. She used to come in here and say things that made my mother twitch." Liesl lowered her voice. "She talked about people watching her. About someone trying to scare her. Once she said she found a paper in the mailbox with no name on it. Just a drawing."

"What kind of drawing?"

"A tree. Or a root. Or maybe both."

Klaus frowned. "Did she tell anyone else?"

"She told me not to repeat it." Liesl folded her arms. "But you're not anyone else. You're the outsider. They're already whispering about you."

He raised an eyebrow. "Are you warning me?"

"I'm just letting you know how much longer your hammering will be welcome."

The warning proved timely.

Later that week, Klaus returned to his cabin to find his garden plot trampled. Not ruined, but stepped through—deliberately. The string line he'd laid to measure furrows had been cut and replaced in a crude knot. A few carrots had been ripped out and tossed into the dirt. Not a word, not a note—just the gesture, petty but precise.

He rebuilt the line, pressed the carrots back into place, and said nothing to the neighbors. But from then on, he kept his tools inside, and his lantern burning later than usual.

The unease extended to church, where Pastor Voltz gave a sermon on "false prophets among us," his eyes scanning the congregation like a man counting sheep before a storm. During communion, no one stood near Klaus. He noticed Herr Schmidt sitting in the third pew, arms crossed, not bothering to kneel when the wine was passed. His eyes were like the edges of slate.

Afterward, Klaus lingered near the well and caught a snatch of conversation from two women.

"…always so polite, but quiet ones can be liars too…"

"…Herr Schmidt said he's asking after things that aren't his concern…"

"…his kind always bring trouble…"

Klaus stepped back before they saw him, the words burrowing deeper than he cared to admit.

That Sunday afternoon, Klaus made an excuse to repair a fence post near the Schmidt property. With his hammer looped through his belt and a bundle of cedar rails slung over his shoulder, he walked the perimeter trail that wound around the orchard. Occasionally, he drove a nail into a post more to maintain the illusion of labor than to serve any practical purpose.

He moved slowly, eyes on the ground. The path Anna would've taken to the creek cut eastward through a stand of ash juniper and curved back toward the riverbank. The area had been lightly searched, he knew, but never combed. And certainly not in the methodical, quiet way he preferred.

Near a low bluff where the trees thickened, Klaus spotted something: an old trail that veered off at a sharp angle behind the Schmidt orchard. The grass had been trampled and slowly begun to rise again, but small signs gave it away—a snapped branch here, the scuff of a bootheel there.

He followed the trail, heart thudding. It ended near a copse of scrub oak clustered along the hill. There, half-buried in dry leaves, stood a limestone marker. It was barely more than a flat rock, angled slightly and worn smooth. But on its surface were two letters—**A.S.**—carved with a blade. Below the initials was a shallow symbol that might've once been a heart, though time and rain had rendered it a hollow curve.

Klaus crouched and ran his fingers across the letters. Fresh. Not new, but not old either. He took a stick and brushed away the leaves, revealing a small arrangement of pebbles—almost like a cairn—

intentionally placed. A child might've played here. Or someone wanted it hidden.

He stood and turned slowly in a circle. No one watched. Not that he could see.

That night, he drew the initials and the heart symbol into his journal. He thought of Liesl's words. A drawing. A root. Or a tree. He closed the journal and sat with it in his lap until the moon rose above the cedar tops, pale and silent.

Two days later, Klaus returned home from a job near the old Baptist church to find his door ajar. Inside, nothing had been taken—but something had been moved. His tools were subtly rearranged. The journal on his desk had been opened. And beside it lay a branch. Not cedar, this time—pecan, bark peeled back to reveal its pale, flesh-like wood. A fresh cut.

Another warning.

He closed the door, locked it from the inside, and leaned his back against it. The walls, once a haven, now felt like a trap. They'd entered his space. Not to steal. Not to destroy. Just to let him know they could.

The next morning, his rain barrel had been drained. His woodpile scattered. He found the carcass of a barn owl nailed to the side of his shed.

At the store, the usual small talk dried up like spilled ale. Men turned their backs to him. Liesl was nowhere to be seen.

When Klaus asked after her, Frau Schmidt gave him a long, cool look.

"She's helping with inventory in the cellar," she said. "Not to be disturbed."

The warning was clear. For a time, at least, Liesl would not be speaking to him.

Klaus paid for his goods in silence and walked out, the bell over the door a shrill accusation behind him.

That evening, wind stirred through the Hill Country like a restless ghost. Klaus sat outside, sharpening his chisel, when he heard it—a voice. Distant. Faint. Carried on the breeze like a child's cry. Then a second voice, lower, almost guttural, responding.

He stood, strained to listen. The sound came from the direction of the old mill.

He grabbed his lantern and a walking stick, hesitated just long enough to slide his knife into his boot, and set off.

The moon lit the trail in patches, silver puddles between shifting shadows. The wind had stirred the cedar, and the smell was thick, cloying. As he neared the mill, the voices stopped.

The structure loomed like a relic, its burned beams black against the sky. The lower walls had been repaired with crude stone, enough to keep livestock out—or in.

Klaus approached the broken door. He paused, listening. Silence.

He entered.

The lantern's glow revealed the same emptiness: beams, dust, collapsed rafters. But this time, something was different.

Footprints. Fresh ones in the dirt—large, booted. And smaller ones, bare.

Klaus followed them around the side of the structure, toward the old stone hearth. There, tucked into a niche between two bricks, was a scrap of paper.

He unfolded it.

The paper was yellowed and torn from a larger sheet. On it, drawn in charcoal, was the same symbol he'd seen on the trail marker: a tree with roots curling like claws beneath.

Beneath the image were two words, scribbled in neat German script.

Du weißt.

You know.

The next morning, Klaus found Liesl sweeping the porch of the general store. Her braid was looser than usual, her knuckles scraped. She looked up and froze when she saw him.

"We shouldn't talk," she said.

"I know. That's why we must."

He stepped closer. "Someone was at the mill last night. I found this."

He showed her the drawing. Her eyes widened. She nodded slowly, then glanced over her shoulder toward the store's window.

"Come back after closing," she whispered. "After dark. The cellar entrance is on the north side."

She turned away before he could speak again.

That night, Klaus waited until the town's lights faded. He slipped through the back lot of the mercantile and found the stone cellar entrance tucked behind stacked crates. A faint light glowed from beneath the door.

He knocked once.

Liesl opened it quickly and pulled him inside. The air was cool and smelled of pickled vegetables and dust.

She lit a second lamp and spoke without preamble.

"Anna told me the same thing before she vanished. She said someone was leaving signs—symbols. Carvings in trees. Stones rearranged in the river. And she said her father had changed."

"Changed how?"

"He stopped asking questions. He stopped talking about the orchard. She found receipts for land her family didn't own. And then someone told her to keep her mouth shut."

"Who?"

"She wouldn't say. Just that it was someone respected."

Klaus nodded slowly. "Did you see her the day she disappeared?"

Liesl hesitated. "She came in here early that morning. Bought a small knife. Said she needed it to 'cut something free.' I thought she meant an animal. Now I don't know."

Klaus felt the hairs on his arms rise.

"Why haven't you said anything?"

"I did," Liesl whispered. "I told Pastor Voltz. He told me to pray. I told the sheriff's deputy. He laughed. Then a week later, I found my dog drowned in the washbasin."

Silence fell between them.

"Why tell me now?" he asked.

"Because they're watching you," Liesl said. "And if you're next, I want you to know you're not alone."

Klaus returned to the mill two days later, this time before dark. He carried a shovel, a lamp, and no illusions.

Inside, he began probing the floor, tapping along the beams for hollow spots. Behind the old fireplace, one stone sounded different. He pried at it.

Behind the stone was a small alcove. Inside lay a bundle of paper wrapped in waxed cloth. He pulled it out carefully and unwrapped it.

Letters.

Dozens of them.

All addressed to Anna Schmidt. None postmarked. All written in the same angular hand.

He opened one and read:

Anna,

I saw the rider again. I know he is watching the orchard. Your father knows more than he admits. They are moving something under the old trail. Meet me at the marker when the moon is high. Burn this letter.

—L.

Klaus froze. The handwriting didn't match Liesl's. But someone had been communicating with Anna. And someone had been warning her.

He gathered the letters and wrapped them tightly. As he stood, he noticed something else—etched on the far wall behind the alcove: a crudely carved spiral, half-buried beneath soot and dust. It looked almost ancient. Like something carved not by a child, but by someone tracing an old memory.

Klaus stepped back. The shape made him dizzy.

He left quickly, locking the door behind him and burying the letters beneath a loose floorboard in his cabin. He would read them later, when his head wasn't spinning.

That night, Klaus stepped out to check the well and saw someone in the field.

A tall man, standing perfectly still near the edge of the orchard.

Watching.

Klaus called out. No response.

He took a step forward, and the figure turned and disappeared into the trees, moving silently despite his size.

Klaus ran to the spot. Nothing remained. Just flattened grass and a faint smell of tobacco.

When he returned to the cabin, a single note was nailed to his door.

Stop digging.

The roots are deeper than you know.

Two days passed. Liesl didn't show up at the store. Her mother claimed she was ill, but wouldn't let Klaus in. He left a small pouch of nails on the porch as a pretense and walked home in a daze.

At sunset, Klaus stood by the riverbank where Anna was last seen. He crouched, staring at the ground, when he noticed something new: a bootprint.

Not his.

Larger. Wider. Fresh.

He followed it a few feet before it vanished into the rocks.

That night, he lit the lamp in his cabin and opened the first of the hidden letters. He read until dawn, hand trembling, jaw clenched.

When he finished, he wrapped them again and whispered a single name: "Anna."

Then he walked into town and found Liesl behind the church, sitting on a stone wall, pale and silent.

He held up one of the letters.

"You knew," he said. "Didn't you?"

Liesl looked up, her eyes rimmed with sleepless shadows.

"I knew enough," she whispered. "But not all of it."

She leaned forward and touched the letter with two fingers.

"They'll kill you too, Klaus. If you get too close."

He looked toward the orchard. Toward the mill. Toward the carved stone with Anna's initials.

"I'm already close."

Chapter 3: An Outsider's Curiosity

Sisterdale did not take kindly to those who stirred its waters.

It had been two days since Klaus found the letters hidden behind the mill hearth—letters written to Anna Schmidt, hinting at hidden dealings, threats, and meetings under moonlight. Two days since Liesl warned him that the town was watching, and that the deeper he dug, the closer he came to being buried alongside the truth.

And now, Sisterdale responded the way small towns do when challenged.

It closed its shutters.

Literally, at first. When Klaus walked into town that Monday morning, heads turned away. Doors that had once stood open with neighborly cheer now shut quietly before he arrived. Conversations that had once paused in welcome now stopped in fear. Pastor Voltz greeted him with a distant nod instead of the usual handshake. Even the children seemed to disappear before he turned the corner.

By the third day, Klaus knew: he was being frozen out.

He had waited long enough.

Klaus rose early, packed the letters—carefully bound and wrapped—in his satchel, and walked the eight dusty miles to Comfort. He arrived before noon, his boots coated in chalky dust, and found the Kendall County substation near the center square.

Sheriff Jeb Stone sat inside with his boots propped on his desk, hat over his eyes, and a toothpick drifting between his lips.

He didn't move as Klaus entered.

"I have evidence," Klaus said in English.

Stone sighed. "Do you now."

Klaus pulled out the stack of letters. "They were hidden behind a fireplace at the old mill."

Stone finally sat up. His expression remained unreadable. He took the top letter and squinted.

"Who's the writer?" he asked.

Klaus shook his head. "Not signed. But addressed to Anna. They show she was scared. Being watched. Maybe blackmailed."

Stone set the letter down and opened another. And another. His eyes scanned faster now, jaw tightening.

Klaus waited.

Finally, Stone leaned back and exhaled slowly. "Well, Mr. Richter, these are… curious, I'll admit that. But none of this is proof. No names. No dates. No crimes."

"She's still missing."

"Correct," Stone said, his voice hardening. "And we have no body, no witness, no motive. I'd have to open an investigation—interview people. Accuse a prominent family with… vague evidence." He gestured at the letters. "This is thin kindling for a very large fire."

Klaus took a step closer. "You're choosing not to act."

"I'm choosing not to waste county resources chasing ghosts."

Stone stood and pointed toward the door. "If you're wise, you'll forget these stories and tend your nails and lumber. Sisterdale doesn't need more outsiders stirring trouble."

Klaus stared at him for a long moment.

Then he gathered the letters and left.

Behind him, Sheriff Stone returned to his chair and placed the toothpick back in his mouth. But the way he drummed his fingers against the desk told Klaus he had hit a nerve.

The walk back felt longer, heavier.

He didn't blame the sheriff entirely. He understood how power protected itself. But the fact remained: if no one else would look, he must.

Klaus spent the next day revisiting each spot mentioned in the letters: the orchard trail, the carved stone, the dry creekbed beyond the Schmidt property. He mapped it all in his journal, overlaying dates from Anna's last known sightings.

He noticed something odd—almost every location aligned along a shallow ridge line that ran northeast through the valley. Not the easiest route, but one that would avoid the main roads and most watchful eyes. A hidden path.

And at the very center of that path?

The Schmidt orchard.

He returned there late in the afternoon under the pretense of offering to fix a fence.

The gate was shut. No one answered his knock. But he could see movement behind the curtains.

He left without a word.

Over the next several days, Klaus began asking more pointed questions—always couched in politeness, always careful.

To the schoolteacher: "Did Anna ever seem distracted?"

To the blacksmith: "You recall seeing her ride that morning?"

To the innkeeper: "Any strangers come through the week before she vanished?"

He heard the same refrain: "Not my business." "Don't know." "She was a good girl." "Best to let it lie."

Some didn't answer at all. Others turned away.

The tighter the walls closed, the more Klaus realized that silence wasn't ignorance.

It was fear.

His breakthrough came on a warm evening near the church. He was repairing a hitching post when he noticed an older woman struggling with her basket.

Frau Renner. Widow. Quiet. Kind. Not especially known for gossip.

He offered to carry her basket home. She accepted, nodding once, eyes sharp despite her years.

As they walked, she said, "You're asking many questions, Herr Richter."

"I only want the truth."

"There are truths," she said softly, "that live better underground."

He said nothing.

At her porch, she leaned in and whispered, "If you must look, go to the ravine north of the orchard. Behind the third spring. But be careful. The ground there… remembers."

Then she took her basket and went inside.

Klaus stood there for a long time.

He went the next morning, just before dawn.

The ravine was hidden behind a tangle of bramble and cedars, half a mile from the Schmidt property. It was dry now, the streambed reduced to scattered stones and lichen.

He followed it until he found the spring. Cold, clear, bubbling from beneath a slab of limestone.

The third spring.

Behind it, the path narrowed. Trees leaned close. He pushed forward and reached a clearing. In its center stood a stone ring—old, moss-covered—once a well or boundary marker.

Around it, the earth had been disturbed.

Not recently. Maybe a month. The grass grew thinner. The air was cooler.

He stepped carefully and noticed something else: a small bone. Not human. Possibly a deer. But burned.

And beside it, half-buried, was a strip of fabric—navy, frayed, and flecked with dried blood.

He dug it out, wrapped it in cloth, and turned back.

That night, he buried the cloth beneath a floorboard beside the letters.

And then he sat for hours, staring at the lantern flame, wondering what else might be buried out there.

Liesl returned to the store the next day.

She looked tired, lips pale, her braid loose. But her eyes still held the same fire.

"I heard what you found," she whispered as he passed her a note inside the store ledger.

"Word travels."

"Even in silence," she said. "They're watching me too."

"You need to stop," he said.

"So do you."

Neither moved.

Finally, Klaus said, "There's more. Letters. Fabric. And bones."

Liesl's face hardened. "Then we don't have much time."

That night, someone knocked at Klaus's door.

He opened it slowly, one hand behind his back on the hammer.

No one stood there.

Only a paper nailed to the frame.

You were warned.
Next time, we bury the truth with you.

Underneath, tied with twine, was a fresh cedar bough.

He burned both in the fireplace without reading them again.

But he didn't sleep.

Two nights later, Klaus returned to the mill.

He waited in the dark, lantern off, hidden behind the door.

At midnight, the voices returned.

Low. Murmuring. Two men.

He stepped out, knife ready.

The voices vanished.

He swung his lantern wide.

No one.

But something new was on the floor: a crate.

Inside: rope, a shovel, and a lantern.

Fresh.

Unused.

He didn't touch it.

He backed away and left.

Klaus began visiting the ravine daily, documenting everything.

He sketched the clearing, measured the disturbed soil, mapped the old trails. He noticed a pattern— each clue led closer to the orchard, circling it like a predator around its prey.

He no longer believed Anna had run away.

He no longer believed it had been an accident.

And he no longer believed the town's silence was born only of fear.

It was something else now.

Complicity.

One morning, Liesl handed him a bundle beneath a sack of flour.

Inside: a note. "Found in my mother's desk."

It was a ledger—receipts for "land surveys," dated two years earlier, paid in cash.

One name appeared on every line: Friedrich Schmidt.

And the land? North of the orchard. The ravine.

All marked private.

All unregistered.

Klaus looked up. "Why?"

Liesl whispered, "Because the land wasn't his to buy."

Klaus walked to the Schmidt house that evening.

Herr Schmidt answered the door with a tired scowl. "You've made yourself known."

Klaus held up the ledger.

Schmidt didn't flinch. "You know nothing."

"I know Anna didn't run away."

"Prove it," Schmidt said. "You have stories. Scraps. But no truth."

"She trusted someone."

Schmidt stepped forward, voice low. "She trusted too many. That was her mistake."

A long pause.

Then he said, almost sadly, "You should leave, Mr. Richter. Before you forget who owns this valley."

Klaus met his eyes.

"Sometimes the land doesn't care who claims it," he said. "It only remembers what was buried."

He turned and walked away.

That night, Klaus awoke to the sound of footsteps.

He grabbed his lamp, swung the door wide.

No one.

But the garden had been torn up again. And beside the well sat a single shoe.

Small. Women's.

He picked it up.

Inside the heel was a scrap of paper:

She saw what was beneath.
So we made her part of it.

Klaus sat on his porch until dawn, the shoe in his lap.

The sun rose, and the hills burned gold.

But Sisterdale, nestled quietly in the shadowed valley, remained silent.

And somewhere beneath its soil, the truth waited, darker and more dangerous than he'd imagined.

But he was no longer a stranger.

He was a reckoning.

Chapter 4: Shadows of the Past

Klaus Richter stood alone beside the ravine. The morning sun crested the eastern ridge, casting long shadows from the twisted oaks. His boots rested near the collapsed cairn. In his hand, he held the worn strip of cloth—a weathered piece of blue cotton, blood-specked and faintly perfumed.

Anna's?

He had no proof. Only the weight in his chest. The same weight he had carried across the Atlantic. The weight of truth too long buried.

A wind stirred the grass at his feet.

He turned toward the trail leading up to the old mill.

The trail was steeper than he remembered.

Klaus climbed slowly, eyes scanning every stone, every gouged root. He knew this route now, knew where the soft soil beneath the cedar gave way to rock. Knew the angle of the hill, the bend of the trail. And he knew he was being watched.

Not just by the birds overhead or the distant deer whose hooves marked the creekbed.

No, this was different. A human presence. Felt but unseen.

He reached the top and crouched near the blackened ruins of the mill. The fire had spared parts of the stone foundation. Burnt beams jutted like broken ribs from the earth. A roofless husk of a building, its silence louder than any shout.

He pulled out the journal Anna had hidden behind the hearth—now dry, its pages fragile but intact. He opened it carefully.

Each page held notes. Names. Symbols. One in particular caught his attention again.

A spiral—etched in charcoal.

He had seen it before. Not just on the page, but carved into stone.

He flipped to the back, where Anna had sketched it again, larger this time, and beneath it, written in hurried script:

"Beneath the mill. Beneath everything."

Klaus searched the floor again. This time he moved with purpose, tapping every plank, every buried stone.

An hour passed.

Then his foot struck hollow wood.

A section near the back wall, beneath a collapsed beam.

He cleared the debris and uncovered a square hatch door, its handle rusted shut. He wedged his chisel beneath it and pried.

With a groan, it opened.

A ladder descended into darkness.

Lantern in one hand, revolver in the other, Klaus climbed down.

The cellar smelled of old smoke, damp wood, and something older—earth and mildew, yes, but also iron. Rust. Or blood.

At the bottom, the lantern flickered against stone walls. Shelves lined with broken jars and tools greeted him. And beyond them, a recess in the wall—bricked over hastily, as if someone meant to forget what was behind it.

He scraped at the mortar with his blade. The brick loosened.

He pulled one free, then another.

Behind them lay bones.

Small ones. Human.

Not just one set.

Several.

He staggered back, heart pounding, bile rising.

There were no markings, no wrappings—only the bones, stacked neatly in a narrow crypt.

He counted at least three skulls.

He dropped to one knee, panting.

Who had buried them here?

And why?

Klaus sat by the wall for a long time.

He remembered something Anna had written:

"The mill is older than the town. Older than the map. They won't speak of what happened. But it's not just about me. It never was."

He rose and returned to the crypt.

He looked for signs—rings, clothing, even remnants of fabric. Anything to date the remains.

Then he found it.

A button. Brass. Embossed with the Prussian eagle.

His blood ran cold.

He had seen that eagle before.

Years ago. In a different courtroom. In a different land.

By the time Klaus returned to his cabin, the sun had long since set. He had wrapped the button in cloth, stowed the journal back beneath the floor, and locked the trapdoor at the mill with a rusted chain.

The air around his cabin felt wrong. Still, expectant.

He stepped onto his porch.

And froze.

The front door was marked.

A spiral, drawn in ash, smeared across the wood like a curse.

Inside, nothing had been stolen.

But everything had been touched.

His bed was unmade.

The photograph of Clara had been turned upside down.

And in the middle of the floor sat a bundle of cedar branches, tied with black string.

Klaus burned them that night.

But the smell lingered.

He did not sleep.

Instead, he sat at his table and opened a second journal—the one he'd carried from Germany. The one no one in Sisterdale had seen.

He turned to the last entry:

"Braunschweig. 1879.
She died believing the law would save her.
I learned it cannot.
Now I carry her voice.
If I speak, I betray the silence.
If I stay silent, I betray her.
So I walk."

He turned the page.

Clara Drechsler smiled back at him from the photograph. Her dark eyes bright, her hand resting on his shoulder, forever frozen in a moment before the lies came.

He remembered the trial. The accusations. The magistrate's condescension.

"You presume too much, Herr Richter. Leave justice to those entrusted with it."

He remembered standing in the rain, the courthouse behind him, watching her mother weep into her shawl.

And then the river.

The final, cruel silence.

He had not saved Clara.

He would not fail again.

The next morning, Klaus took the button to Liesl.

They sat behind the store, hidden from view.

When she saw it, her eyes widened.

"That's from the regiment," she whispered. "My grandfather had one."

He nodded. "It was found in the cellar beneath the mill. With bones. Children."

She swallowed. "How old?"

"Old enough to be forgotten."

"Or buried."

They sat in silence.

Then Liesl said, "There's something else. I didn't know if I should show you."

She pulled a small notebook from her satchel. "Anna left this at the store two weeks before she vanished. She said if anything happened to her, I should give it to someone who wouldn't look away."

Klaus took the book.

Inside, Anna had drawn more than symbols. She had drawn faces. Maps. And a single page with names:

- Schmidt

- Voltz

- Reiter

- Kessler

Klaus recognized them all. Prominent men. Influential.

Beside each name was a date.

Some recent. Some very old.

And one, circled in ink: **May 2, 1864.**

Klaus returned to the mill and began digging.

Not in the cellar. But behind it, where the foundation curved around the back wall.

The soil there was different. Loose. Recently disturbed.

After an hour of digging, he hit stone.

A flat slab, engraved with initials: "R.K. 1864"

He lifted it.

Beneath, wrapped in oilcloth, lay a bound sheaf of papers.

A diary.

Klaus read by lamplight as the sun set over Sisterdale.

The diary belonged to a woman named Rebekka Kessler.

The first entry dated April 1864.

"They have taken my son to the river. Said he saw what should not be seen."

"Pastor Voltz told me to keep silent. That the town must survive. But I cannot. I will bury this with my hands if I must."

"If they find this, I am already gone."

The final entry, dated May 2:

"The fire is lit. They call it a purification. They burn the mill to cleanse it. But I know the truth. They burn it to bury."

That night, Klaus found a fire lit outside his cabin.

Not burning. Smoldering.

In the middle: the photograph of Clara. Torn in half.

And a word, scrawled in ash on the ground:

"Run."

He didn't.

Two nights later, Liesl was found unconscious behind the church.

Bruised. Frightened. Shaking.

She had no memory of the attack. Only a voice, whispering, "Leave it."

Klaus sat beside her at the doctor's house, hands clenched.

When she woke, she met his gaze.

"They know we know."

That night, Klaus met with Pastor Voltz.

He laid the diary on the table between them.

Voltz looked at it, then at Klaus.

His face aged in seconds.

"I was not there," he whispered. "I only heard the stories. The night of the fire, the children who vanished. The land dispute."

Klaus said nothing.

"I told myself it was legend. Old blood feuds. But I knew. Deep down."

"You stayed silent."

"I feared what would happen if the truth came out."

"It already has."

Voltz nodded. "Then you must finish it."

Klaus returned to the mill.

He opened the trapdoor one last time.

This time, he lit every lantern he brought, bathing the cellar in light.

He placed the diary, the letters, the bones— everything—on the floor.

Then he sat.

And waited.

He knew someone would come.

Someone always came when silence was threatened.

And he would be ready.

Chapter 5: Unlikely Allies and Hidden Enemies

The town of Sisterdale had changed.

Not in a way most people could name, not in the streets or the trees or the shadows across the limestone hills. But in the way the town breathed. In the way windows stayed shuttered longer in the morning. In the way children glanced over their shoulders without knowing why. In the way whispers clung to corners and stilled the air when Klaus Richter entered a room.

It was not fear that had taken hold of the valley.

It was anticipation.

The quiet, coiled moment before something breaks.

Klaus sat in the cool dark of the abandoned mill, the cellar lamp flickering low beside him. He had returned each night for three days, waiting. Watching. Leaving the door unlocked. Baiting the silence.

On the fourth night, someone entered.

Footsteps. Light. Barefoot. Measured.

He raised the lantern.

Liesl.

"You shouldn't be here," he whispered.

"I couldn't sleep," she said. "I saw the fire you left burning and followed it."

Klaus didn't speak. He handed her a letter—one of Anna's. The one marked with the spiral.

Liesl read it in silence, lips tight.

Then she handed him a folded paper of her own.

"A map," she said. "Drawn from memory. Anna once told me there was a place behind the Schmidt farm—an old stone cellar built before the war. Her father never spoke of it, but she followed him there once. Said it looked like a root cellar, but it was always locked from the inside."

Klaus studied the paper. "How sure are you?"

"I was never sure," she said. "Until you started digging. Until they tried to silence me."

Klaus nodded slowly. "Then we find it. Tonight."

They left after midnight, walking the ridge line to avoid being seen from the main road. The moon was sharp, cold as bone. When they reached the Schmidt farm, Klaus stopped and studied the land.

The orchard looked different in moonlight. The trees less orderly. The rows more like ribs than fruit-bearing limbs. As if the land itself were hiding something beneath.

Behind the barn, nestled against the bluff, they found it.

A square slab of stone, half-covered in brush. A rusted iron handle set into its face.

Klaus knelt, ran his fingers along the edge. Dirt had been packed tightly around it. Recently disturbed.

He pulled.

It didn't budge.

Then Liesl pointed. "There."

A small iron ring, half-buried nearby. They dug, uncovering a mechanism—cleverly designed. A counter-lever system that released the lock with a twist.

The slab shifted. Groaned. Then lifted.

A short set of stairs descended into dark.

They exchanged a glance.

Then Klaus took the lead.

The cellar was deeper than it had any right to be.

Stone walls, smooth. Purposeful. Not farmhand work.

And at the far end—shelves. Papers. Boxes. Maps. Records.

In the center, a wooden table. Clean. Recently used.

On it, a set of plans. Land surveys. Boundary claims. And a single name signed in the corner: **Frederick H. Schmidt.**

"Land ownership," Liesl whispered. "But not the kind you register with the county."

Klaus sifted through the documents.

Hidden titles. Dated signatures. Dozens of names scratched out and replaced with others.

"Forgery," he murmured. "Or worse—forced sales. This isn't just about Anna. It's about the land."

At the bottom of one stack, a list of initials.

K.R.
A.S.
L.G.

Liesl's breath caught.

"My initials."

Klaus folded the page. "They've been keeping track of us. Of everyone."

Then he paused.

Something glinted at the edge of the shelf.

A pendant.

Silver. Shaped like a star. The same Anna had worn the day she vanished.

Klaus held it in his hand. It was still warm.

"Someone's been here recently."

Liesl stepped back. "We need to go."

But Klaus stayed frozen, staring at the pendant.

"No," he said. "We need to stay."

Outside, a twig snapped.

Klaus extinguished the lantern. Liesl pressed her back against the stone wall, eyes wide.

Footsteps passed above.

Slow. Heavy.

Then a voice, low and humming.

A tune. Old. German.

Klaus recognized it instantly.

Die Gedanken sind frei.

His mother's lullaby.

The same one she had sung in Braunschweig as she tucked him in, long before trials and ships and exile.

The footsteps faded.

But the song remained.

They waited another hour before leaving.

Back at Klaus's cabin, they spread the documents across the table. Liesl lit two lamps and poured coffee with shaking hands.

"We're not just dealing with a missing girl," she said. "This is a conspiracy."

Klaus nodded. "A theft."

"Of what?"

"Of truth. Of land. Of lives."

He pointed to a map dated 1865. The same section of land behind the ravine—now marked as Schmidt property—had once been designated as a public trust.

A deed signed by Rebekka Kessler.

"She tried to preserve it," Klaus said. "They buried her for it."

Liesl sat down hard. "How many people know?"

Klaus didn't answer.

Because he already knew the answer.

Too many.

And not one of them trustworthy.

Over the next week, Klaus and Liesl worked in secret. At night, they returned to the hidden cellar, documenting everything. By day, they acted as if nothing had changed. Klaus fixed roofs. Liesl stocked shelves. They played their roles, waiting.

But the town knew.

They felt it in every glance. Every too-long pause. Every carefully measured word.

On Thursday, someone left a dead crow nailed to Klaus's door.

On Friday, the town's paper printed a short article:

"Newcomer Raises Alarm with Unfounded Accusations."

Beneath it: his name.

And an editorial by Pastor Voltz.

Klaus stared at the page, betrayed.

"He's one of them," Liesl said.

"No," Klaus whispered. "He's being forced."

"Does it matter?"

Klaus looked out the window.

"They know we're close."

That night, Klaus found his cabin door ajar.

Inside, nothing was missing—but every drawer had been emptied. His journal had been slashed with a knife. Pages shredded. Ink spilled across the floor.

On the wall above his bed, drawn in charcoal:

"The roots remember."

Below it: the spiral.

Liesl sat with him in silence.

Then she handed him something new.

A journal.

Anna's.

"I found it behind a false panel in the store," she said. "I think she meant you to have it."

Klaus opened the first page.

"If I disappear, don't believe them.
The orchard is the key.
Beneath the third tree."

They returned to the orchard the next night.

Third row. Third tree.

An old pecan, its bark scarred with age.

Klaus dug at the base.

After ten minutes, his blade struck wood.

A small box.

Inside: letters. Photographs. A ledger.

But most shocking—a photograph of Anna, taken recently. Smiling. Dated two weeks after her disappearance.

"She's alive," Liesl whispered.

But Klaus said nothing.

He was staring at the second photo.

A man.

Dark eyes. Full beard.

Herr Schmidt.

But younger.

And beside him—a woman. Not Helene.

Clara.

Klaus stormed into Pastor Voltz's office the next morning, the photo clutched in his fist.

"You knew," he said.

Voltz looked up, eyes haunted.

"I suspected."

"Why didn't you say anything?"

Voltz exhaled. "Because they threatened the church. The orphans. The sick. I made a choice."

"You chose wrong."

Voltz nodded.

"I know."

He slid a small key across the desk.

"To the church's old records. In the bell tower. You'll find what you need there."

Klaus took it.

And walked out.

In the bell tower, Klaus found the records.

Buried beneath old hymnals, behind the rusted gears of the bell, he found a ledger from 1864.

Baptismal entries. Land deeds. Names crossed out in red ink.

And one name added in the margin.

Clara Drechsler.

Beside it: "Relocated. Silent. Paid."

Klaus sat down hard.

She had survived.

For a time.

They had silenced her with money. Or threats.

And then made her disappear again.

Just like Anna.

That night, Klaus lit every lantern in the mill.

He placed the photo of Clara on the table. Beside it, Anna's journal. Rebekka's diary. The forged maps. The ledgers.

He placed them in order.

Like a trial.

Like an offering.

And waited.

He knew they would come.

Because justice does not sleep forever.

And secrets—no matter how deep—will always claw their way to the surface.

Chapter 6: The Web Tightens

The air in Sisterdale had changed again.

It was no longer merely watchful or wary—it was clenched. Like the breath before a scream, the moment before a dam gives way. The town moved slower, as if time itself had narrowed. People walked in tighter groups. Windows stayed shut even on warm mornings. The store closed early. Pastor Voltz no longer gave his weekly sermons.

And the eyes.

Everywhere, eyes.

On Klaus.

On Liesl.

Watching.

Waiting.

Klaus stood in the bell tower at St. Peter's, the ledger open in his hands, the brittle paper softening beneath the rising sun. The name written there—**Clara Drechsler**—burned in his vision. He hadn't spoken it aloud in years. He had carried her loss like a wound, one he believed to be personal, contained in Germany.

But here it was again.

Here.

Buried beneath the quiet steeple of a Texas church.

Beside it: a false birth record. A scribbled date. A notation—"relocated for the good of the valley."

He ran his thumb over the faded ink.

What did they mean? Had Clara been taken? Had she come here to hide? Had she uncovered the same secret—and been silenced?

Liesl climbed the stairs behind him, out of breath.

"They're talking about you," she said.

"I imagine they are."

"No," she said. "Not like before. They're saying you've hurt someone. That you lied about Clara. That you're the one who took Anna."

Klaus turned sharply. "What?"

"They're calling a meeting. At the town hall. Tonight."

The sun had not yet reached its peak when the accusations began.

Klaus walked into town for nails. At the store, two men stood near the door, arms crossed. One, a rancher named Otto Reiter, stepped forward.

"We'd like a word, Herr Richter."

Klaus paused. "I'm listening."

Otto's face was carefully blank. "Where were you the night Anna disappeared?"

"Here. Helping the Müllers repair their barn. I told Sheriff Stone."

"I heard otherwise," Otto said.

From behind him, a third man added, "You've been snooping. Digging. Making trouble. Maybe you're the one who made her vanish."

Klaus didn't flinch. "I've been looking for answers. You should be asking who benefits from her disappearance."

Otto spat. "We don't take kindly to strangers accusing our own."

Another man stepped forward. "Maybe it's time we reminded you of that."

Klaus didn't wait. He turned and walked out, the press of suspicion behind him like a tide.

The town hall was crowded that night.

Every family was represented. The benches filled quickly. Women clutched shawls. Men leaned forward, hands on knees. Pastor Voltz stood near the front, silent. Even the sheriff had returned, seated by the stove, arms crossed.

Klaus stood near the back. Alone.

Herr Schmidt stepped forward to speak.

"We've welcomed many into our valley," he began. "But some come with baggage. With secrets. And with destruction."

He turned, slowly, scanning the room.

"Anna is gone. And still, no answers. No evidence. No progress. But we have someone in our midst who stirs old ghosts, who breaks into homes, who digs where he should not."

Murmurs rippled through the crowd.

"Last week, he accused me of forgery," Schmidt continued. "Before that, he harassed my wife. He has lied, stolen, and disturbed the peace."

Liesl tried to rise, but someone blocked her path.

Schmidt raised his hand.

"I propose we turn him over to the county. Let Sheriff Stone take him in for questioning. And let us restore calm to this town."

All eyes turned to Klaus.

He stepped forward.

And unrolled the photographs.

Clara.

Anna.

The land surveys.

The fake deeds.

"This is your calm?" he said. "Buried girls and buried truths?"

Schmidt laughed. "Forged. All of it."

Klaus turned to Voltz.

"Tell them."

Voltz said nothing.

Schmidt smiled. "Even your allies know the truth."

Sheriff Stone stood.

"I think we'd best escort Mr. Richter to Comfort."

Two deputies appeared at Klaus's side.

The jail in Comfort was small. One cell. One window.

Klaus sat on the cot, bruised from the rough handling.

Sheriff Stone stood outside the bars, arms crossed.

"You should've left well enough alone."

"There are bodies under that mill," Klaus said.

Stone shrugged. "Bodies don't talk."

Klaus reached into his shirt and pulled out a small item he'd kept hidden: the silver pendant from Anna's necklace.

He tossed it between the bars.

Stone caught it. His eyes narrowed.

Klaus said, "That's not from a body. That's from a girl who's alive."

Stone stared at him.

Then left without a word.

Back in Sisterdale, Liesl acted.

She broke into the church and recovered the ledgers.

She rode to the Müller farm and took their sworn statement that Klaus had been there the night Anna disappeared.

She visited the old cellar one final time.

There, she found something Klaus had missed.

A handkerchief.

Monogrammed.

A.S.

And beneath it, fresh dirt.

Not long dug.

She unearthed a small notebook.

Anna's final journal.

In it, a name.

Kessler.

And the word: *springhouse*.

Liesl rode to Comfort before sunrise.

She stormed into the jail, notebook in hand.

Stone tried to wave her off.

But she handed him the journal.

He read.

Paused.

Then unlocked the cell.

"Don't make me regret this," he said to Klaus.

Klaus stood.

"I already regret it for you."

They rode back at full gallop.

Behind the Schmidt property, beyond the orchard, near a trickling spring, they found it.

An old limestone building, half-collapsed.

Inside, a cot.

A jug of water.

Clothes.

And Anna.

Alive.

Weak. Pale. But alive.

She blinked at the light.

Then whispered, "I thought I was going to die here."

Anna's story poured out in pieces.

Her father had found the old deeds.

He had forced people off their land quietly, forging signatures, burning records.

When Anna confronted him, he locked her away—first at the springhouse, then moved her when people asked too many questions.

She'd escaped two days earlier and returned here, hoping someone would come.

Liesl held her hand.

"You're safe now."

Klaus turned to Stone.

"You have your motive."

Stone nodded.

"We have our villain."

That evening, Herr Schmidt was arrested.

The town was stunned.

Some protested.

Most were silent.

But when Anna stepped into the church that Sunday—alive—Sisterdale changed again.

Not back to what it was.

But into something new.

Something cleaner.

Klaus stood at the edge of town, watching the hills.

Liesl joined him.

"It's over," she said.

He shook his head.

"It's only beginning."

Chapter 7: A Traitor in the Ranks

Sisterdale did not celebrate its liberation.

The day after Herr Schmidt's arrest, the town woke to silence—not the heavy, watchful silence that had hovered over it for months, but a stunned quiet. As if the townspeople were waiting for the next page to turn and weren't sure whether they wanted to read what came next.

Anna remained in hiding at the parsonage. Sheriff Stone, unusually efficient, arranged her formal statement and delivered the first charges to the county seat by week's end. Testimonies were collected. Maps seized. A deputy was dispatched from Boerne to collect the land deeds and begin sorting the legal tangle Schmidt had left behind.

Klaus and Liesl should have felt victorious.

But neither did.

Victory, they realized, carried its own kind of weight.

And enemies often hid deeper than the first layer.

"You have to publish it," Liesl said.

They sat at the general store late one evening, poring over a bundle of papers. Klaus had compiled every document—Anna's letters, the Kessler diary, the forged ledgers, even his own notes. The bundle sat before them like kindling.

"If it stays here, it dies here," Liesl added. "They'll bury it again."

Klaus nodded slowly. "Austin has a newspaper. *The German Free Press.* One of the few that might print it without fear."

"Then we take it to them."

Klaus glanced at the clock. "We need protection. If someone finds out before we get it there…"

Liesl stood and paced. "We need a judge. Someone with reach. With authority beyond the county."

"There's a circuit judge coming through next week. Rides the Boerne-Sisterdale-Fredericksburg route."

"Judge Ransom," she said. "He's fair."

Klaus hesitated. "Then we show him everything. Let him hear it from Anna. And if he won't act, we go to Austin."

They agreed.

Three days. That's all they needed.

On the second day, a stranger arrived in Sisterdale.

Tall. Pale coat. Dusty boots. Black gloves, though the weather was warm.

He rode in on a dark gelding and tied it outside the church before walking straight into the general store.

Klaus and Liesl watched from the back office.

"Who is he?" Liesl whispered.

"Don't know. But he's not lost."

Frau Schmidt greeted the man like an old friend—though Klaus noted the stiffness in her posture, the way her eyes never quite met his.

Later that night, the stranger was seen speaking with several men outside the schoolhouse—Otto Reiter among them.

By morning, rumors had returned.

That Anna's story was false.

That she'd made it up to punish her father.

That Klaus had forged the letters.

That Liesl was in love with him and blinded by it.

Klaus barely slept.

They were being outmaneuvered—again.

The third night, Liesl didn't come to the meeting place behind the church.

Klaus waited an hour.

Then two.

He returned to the cabin, where Anna was waiting with Pastor Voltz.

"She didn't return home," Anna said, voice tight. "She left after supper."

Klaus's stomach turned.

He turned to Voltz. "Find the sheriff."

They spent the night searching—past the orchard, down by the creek, even the mill.

Nothing.

Just before dawn, a rider approached the cabin.

It was the stranger.

He dismounted, removed his gloves, and handed Klaus a folded sheet of paper.

Klaus opened it.

Inside was a confession—written in Liesl's hand.

"I lied. Anna was never in danger. Klaus coerced me.

He forged the evidence.
I recant everything."

Klaus stared at the page.

Anna gasped.

"She didn't write this."

"No," Klaus said. "She was forced."

That afternoon, Sheriff Stone returned to Sisterdale with two deputies.

"This is getting out of hand," he told Klaus. "Judge Ransom arrives tomorrow. We'll let him sort it out."

But Klaus heard it in his voice—resignation. Or fear.

He was losing support fast.

That evening, he returned to the mill.

Everything was gone.

The papers. The maps. Even the bones.

Only a charred circle remained where the crates had stood.

He dropped to his knees and sifted through the ashes.

The spiral was drawn there again—this time in salt.

Not a warning.

A signature.

Just after midnight, someone tapped at Klaus's window.

It was Anna.

She held a scrap of cloth.

Liesl's red hair ribbon.

Tied around it was a note—scribbled, shaky:

"Under the floorboards. I'm sorry."

They returned to the general store and searched beneath the back office.

In the crawl space, wrapped in oilskin, was a second bundle—hidden there by Liesl before her disappearance.

Inside: a journal. Her real one.

Dozens of pages. Notes. Observations. And a final message:

"If I disappear, they've taken me.
The man in white is their enforcer.
They call him Der Bote—The Messenger.
He answers to no one but them.
Don't stop.
Whatever they say, don't stop."

Klaus closed the journal and turned to Anna.

"We bring this to the judge tomorrow."

Judge Elias Ransom was a wiry man in a rumpled coat with sharp eyes and a habit of twirling his watch chain when he was deep in thought. He arrived in Sisterdale with a young clerk and a tin lockbox filled with ledgers.

He met Klaus and Anna in the parsonage just after lunch.

Klaus laid out the documents.

The journal. The letters. The hidden deeds.

Anna gave her testimony again.

The judge listened.

Took notes.

Asked questions.

Then sat back, hands steepled.

"And what became of the girl? Liesl?"

"Taken. We believe by force."

Ransom nodded. "You've done well bringing this forward. I'll need to conduct depositions. Interviews. It won't be swift."

"We don't have time," Klaus said. "They're burying it again. Right now."

Ransom looked him square in the eye.

"Then make it loud."

At the judge's request, a town meeting was held the next morning.

This time, Klaus stood in the front.

Judge Ransom sat beside him.

Anna, pale but steady, spoke first.

She described her father's actions. The fake land claims. Her imprisonment. The threats.

Then Klaus presented the documents.

The forged deeds.

The hidden records.

The diaries.

Gasps rippled through the crowd.

Otto Reiter stood and tried to interrupt.

Then the judge raised a hand.

"I have seen enough to warrant a full inquiry," he said. "Effective immediately, I am seizing all land documents in Sisterdale for review. Anyone interfering will face charges.”

Then, he paused.

“I also want the man in white brought in. Alive.”

Klaus spoke next.

“I will find him. And I will bring Liesl home.”

That night, Klaus returned to the place it all began: the ravine.

There, beneath the third spring, he found a new trail.

Trampled.

Recently used.

He followed it west—into the cedar.

For hours.

Until he saw it: a cabin. Hidden. Stone chimney. One horse tied outside.

Inside, through a cracked shutter, he saw her.

Liesl.

Bound. Silent.

And across from her, cleaning a knife, was Der Bote.

The Messenger.

Klaus waited until moonlight gave him cover.

Then he moved.

The door creaked.

The man looked up—

Too late.

Klaus struck with the shovel.

The man staggered, hissed, reached for his gun—

And Anna stepped from behind the trees and shot him in the leg.

He screamed.

Klaus disarmed him.

Then turned to Liesl, cut her free.

Her first words were a whisper.

"I didn't break."

They returned just after dawn.

The Messenger, bleeding but alive, was placed in the custody of the judge.

Liesl was escorted to the parsonage.

And Klaus?

He walked alone to the orchard.

He stood beneath the third tree.

And let himself breathe—for the first time in weeks.

But he knew this wasn't over.

Because roots run deep.

And some trees, no matter how tall, grow from poisoned ground.

Chapter 8: The Reckoning

The sky over Sisterdale was a deep, unsettled gray the morning Klaus Richter stood again before the mill.

The clouds hung heavy, close to the hills, like breath just before a scream. The wind carried no birdsong, only the restless stirring of leaves. It felt like the valley was holding its breath.

The reckoning had come.

And Klaus knew there was no more hiding.

No more whispers.

No more shadows.

The truth was clawing to the surface—bloody, furious, and undeniable.

Judge Ransom had sent word to Fredericksburg for a formal inquest. Sheriff Stone, finally shaken into real action, stationed two deputies at the Schmidt estate and placed Anna under protective watch in the parsonage. Liesl, though bruised and weak from her captivity, was helping the judge sort through the last of the land documents. And Klaus—he was watching the orchard.

He knew it was not over.

The Messenger, Der Bote, had been arrested. But he wasn't talking.

And the real power behind it all—the mind that had orchestrated everything—still hadn't shown its face.

That power had used Schmidt.

Had silenced Clara.

Had buried the Kessler name.

And had tried to turn the whole town into accomplices.

Klaus wasn't looking for justice anymore.

He was hunting.

It came from Pastor Voltz.

That afternoon, as rain threatened on the horizon, Voltz summoned Klaus to the bell tower once more.

He looked older. As though the truth had drained him.

He handed Klaus a letter.

"I found this hidden beneath the baptismal registry. Dated 1864. Rebekka Kessler's final testament. It was never delivered. She meant it for the original founder of the town—a man named Johann Keller."

Klaus read it aloud.

"They meet beneath the stone church. In the vault. Not to worship—but to sign. They call it protection. I call it a grave. If I die, know that the vault is the root. Everything else is branches."

Beneath it was a name Klaus had never seen connected to the conspiracy before.

August Reiter.

Otto's grandfather.

Klaus looked up.

Voltz nodded. "Otto inherited everything. The land. The documents. And the secrets."

Otto Reiter had been quiet since Schmidt's arrest.

Too quiet.

While others protested or whispered, he simply withdrew—shut his store, tended his fields, declined all interviews.

Now Klaus understood why.

He wasn't protecting Schmidt.

He was protecting himself.

Klaus rode to the Reiter property.

Otto met him on the porch, rifle across his knees.

"I wondered when you'd come," he said.

"You're the last name," Klaus said. "The one no one mentioned."

Otto nodded slowly. "Because they know better."

"You started all this."

"My grandfather did. I only kept it from falling apart."

Klaus stepped closer. "By bribing, forging, killing."

"I preserved Sisterdale," Otto said, eyes flashing. "You think this town survives on good intentions? It survives on control. On blood when necessary."

"You took Clara. You buried the Kesslers. You used Schmidt as your puppet."

"Schmidt was eager. He thought he was leading. I let him believe it."

"You sent Der Bote."

"I sent many."

Klaus clenched his fists. "Then end it. Confess. Let the judge see."

Otto stood slowly, rifle in hand.

"I'd rather burn it all down."

It began that night.

Smoke rose from the valley at midnight—first from the general store, then from the mill, then from the church.

Three fires.

One message.

Klaus ran through the rain-soaked streets, shouting warnings. Buckets were passed. Bells rang.

The town awoke in chaos.

But even as they fought to save what they could, Klaus knew the true fire was yet to come.

Otto had vanished.

And Anna was gone.

She had been taken from the parsonage window— no signs of struggle. Only muddy footprints, leading west.

Klaus and Liesl followed them to the hills.

At sunrise, they found the hidden passage behind the old springhouse—a tunnel once used by Unionists fleeing the war.

They descended.

Torch in hand, Klaus moved silently through the narrow stone corridor, the earth closing around him like a tomb.

Then they saw her.

Anna.

Bound to a wooden chair, eyes wide.

Otto stood behind her, pistol in hand.

"No closer," he said.

Klaus raised his hands.

"She's not your enemy."

"She's my legacy," Otto hissed. "Proof of what happens when you let truth take root."

"You've already lost," Klaus said. "The judge knows. The town knows."

"They'll forget. They always do."

Klaus took another step.

Otto raised the gun—

But Liesl, unseen, tackled him from behind.

The gun fired—once.

Stone cracked.

Then Otto lay pinned, groaning, beneath her.

Klaus freed Anna.

The three of them stumbled back into the light.

At the inquest three days later, Anna testified again.

So did Liesl.

Pastor Voltz. Judge Ransom.

And finally, Otto—dragged into the courthouse in shackles, his voice low and bitter.

"Yes," he said. "We built Sisterdale on a lie. And the lie served us well."

He smiled at Klaus.

"But you won't last. Heroes never do."

Later that week, as Klaus walked home from the orchard, a final blow fell.

One of Otto's men—hidden, desperate, loyal—stepped from the shadows with a knife.

Klaus fought.

He bled.

But he survived.

The attacker fled, caught hours later with a map and one last order:

"Finish the carpenter."

The town had turned.

But the roots still twisted.

Otto Reiter died two weeks later.

Poison.

Self-inflicted.

He left no note.

Only an open ledger, and a spiral drawn in ink across the final page.

With Reiter dead and Schmidt imprisoned, the conspiracy collapsed.

Land claims were reexamined.

Records restored.

Rebekka Kessler's name was carved into a new stone at the church.

Clara's story—finally told—was published in *The German Free Press* under the title:

"The Carpenter of Sisterdale."

Chapter 9: Ashes and Rebirth

The flames were gone, but the smoke lingered.

It crept into the cracks of Sisterdale's buildings, into the folds of blankets and coats, into the memories of those who had watched their secrets burn beneath the rain-slicked sky. It mingled with guilt and with grief. The kind of grief that didn't shout, didn't weep, but curled itself like a question at the back of the throat.

What now?

The general store had been gutted. The roof had collapsed and the shelves lay in charred ruin, tins melted together, flour blackened into cinders. Liesl stood in the rubble that had once been her life's routine. Her hands were black with soot as she sifted through what could be salvaged.

Pastor Voltz and a handful of others worked beside her. They pulled up the floorboards, saved what they could. The community had gathered—not in protest this time, but in mourning.

The mill, too, was gone. Nothing remained of the ledgers, the false maps, the twisted bones of buried crimes. In one sense, it was a cleansing. In another, it was a second burial.

The church had survived—barely. The roof sagged, scorched on one side. But the bell still rang, cracked though it was, and every evening it tolled a single note.

For the dead.

For the lost.

For the truth that finally, painfully, had been spoken.

Klaus returned to his cabin and sat in silence.

The table he'd built now bore a strange kind of weight. On it lay three items: a small black journal, a broken shard of pottery from the mill, and the photograph of the woman he had left behind in Germany.

He picked up the journal. Liesl's notes. Her careful documentation. Her words were what had turned whispers into evidence, memory into testimony. She had risked everything.

And yet the town remained divided.

Some saw him as the man who had burned the rot away. Others called him the one who brought the fire.

He had learned not to listen to either.

He went to the orchard the next morning and resumed his work—not for wages now, but for the rhythm. He dug trenches for irrigation. Rebuilt fences. Repaired a roof that had buckled under ash. The Müller children watched him from a distance, whispering. The youngest offered him a peach.

He accepted it with a nod.

Clara Kessler was given a proper memorial.

A stone marker, whitewashed and unadorned, was placed beneath the twisted oak at the back of the old cemetery. Liesl read a passage from Psalms. Pastor Voltz led the hymn. Anna stood silent, a bouquet of wildflowers in her hands.

When the service ended, people lingered.

"I knew her," someone said.

"She used to sing with the choir," said another.

No one had spoken her name in twenty years.

Now they did.

Not just hers.

Rebekka. Johann. Even those whose names were written only in ashes and rumor. Sisterdale, like any town, had been built by more than its founding fathers. It had been built by hands no one wanted to name.

Now those names were carved in stone.

And some, Klaus knew, would never be.

Liesl moved into the schoolhouse while the store was rebuilt.

By choice, she remained there—at first to organize supplies for the town's children, then as an impromptu teacher. She was only twenty, but when she spoke, people listened. Her voice was low and clear, and when children asked questions, she answered them all. Even the hard ones.

"Why did Mr. Schmidt lie?"

"Why did they hide the girl?"

"What does *justice* mean?"

She never flinched.

When the *German Free Press* requested an interview with Klaus, he declined. He sent them to Liesl instead. Her article ran under the title:

"Truth and Timber: Rebuilding Sisterdale."

It was read across the Hill Country.

It changed nothing overnight.

But it began a new chapter.

Anna stayed in Sisterdale until the trial.

Her testimony helped convict the last remaining conspirators—three men who had falsified deeds and threatened witnesses. The trial was short. The verdicts unanimous.

When the court adjourned, she did not cry.

She met Klaus in front of the courthouse. The spring sun lit her auburn hair.

"I'm leaving," she said.

"Where?"

"San Antonio. I want to become a nurse."

Klaus smiled. "You'll be good at it."

"I owe you."

"You don't owe me anything."

She leaned forward and hugged him, her voice soft at his ear. "You saved me."

"No," he whispered. "You saved yourself."

She turned and walked away.

Klaus watched her disappear into the dust and did not follow.

The trees budded in April.

The creek, which had run sluggish with soot and ash, cleared itself with time. The fish returned. Birds, too. The valley, stubborn and unbroken, remembered its old songs.

One morning, Klaus saw a stranger ride into town— new to the land, eyes wide, boots scuffed by the road. The same look he had worn a year ago. The man asked for directions. Klaus gave them.

Before he could leave, the man turned and asked, "Is this a good place?"

Klaus thought for a moment.

"It's a place that's trying to be."

In May, a letter arrived from Germany.

It was from Klaus's sister.

She had heard rumors—of a trial, a missing girl, a German carpenter. She wrote in cautious language, but the emotion was unmistakable.

"They say you have done something good.
Something brave.
I hope that's true."

She enclosed a photograph.

The family home, still standing.

A cherry tree in bloom.

Klaus stared at it for a long time.

Then tucked it beside the photo of the woman he had once loved.

Two lives.

One never lived.

One he was still writing.

The town held a festival in June.

Not to celebrate.

To acknowledge.

They planted trees in the square—four of them. One for Clara. One for Rebekka. One for Anna, though she had left. And one without a name.

"For the ones we don't know," Liesl said.

Klaus stood at the back of the crowd.

He did not speak.

He didn't need to.

As the final song faded, Pastor Voltz approached him.

"We've been wrong before," the pastor said. "We didn't see what was in front of us."

Klaus looked at the man. "Will you see it now?"

Voltz nodded. "I will try."

Liesl took over the store that summer.

The schoolhouse remained open.

Children returned.

So did travelers.

The valley slowly filled again—with new families, with laughter, with the cautious rebuilding of trust.

Klaus continued his work.

He built fences. Repaired tools. Constructed a small library beside the church.

But something in him had changed.

He no longer sought silence.

Now, he sought *clarity*.

He told his story.

Not often. But enough.

And when people asked why he had done it—why he had risked everything—he said only:

"Because someone had to."

And most people nodded.

Some didn't.

That, he knew, would never change.

One evening, Klaus climbed the hill above the town and looked down.

Sisterdale shimmered in the gold light of dusk.

Smoke rose from chimneys.

Children played by the creek.

The mill's charred remains had been cleared— replaced by an open field of wildflowers.

Liesl's store glowed with lantern light.

Peace, he thought.

Not perfect.

But real.

He sat beneath an old cedar, pulled out his journal, and began to write.

"Peace is not the absence of violence.
It is the refusal to let violence write the ending.
We choose our ending."

He closed the book.

And watched the valley breathe.

Chapter 10: The Quiet Hill Country

The cicadas sang.

The summer heat had mellowed by late August, and the hills above Sisterdale wore their usual haze of gold and dust. Klaus Richter stood at the edge of his porch, sharpening a chisel. He paused to listen—birds in the trees, a dog barking somewhere down the valley, a hammer striking rhythmically against wood.

Life, he realized, had returned to its patterns.

But nothing was quite the same.

The town remembered.

Not loudly, not in parades or speeches, but in quieter ways. The general store bore a new name now—*Liesl's Mercantile*. She had rebuilt it with her own hands, with the help of neighbors and a donation box placed in Fredericksburg. It stood where the old store had burned, but it had more windows now. More light.

Children ran in and out of it each morning on their way to school.

Liesl taught reading on Thursdays, bookkeeping on Fridays. She held discussion nights every second

Sunday. People came. Not just for goods, but for advice, for stories, for news from beyond the valley.

Klaus visited often. Never long, but often.

Their friendship had changed, ripened into something steady, respectful. She had become the voice of the town. He had become its hands.

The orchard behind his home now bore fruit.

Plums, mostly. A few sour apples. He gave most away. The orchard had become a gathering place on Saturdays—a picnic spot, a place for songs and shared labor. Children chased each other between the rows. Parents brought quilts. Someone always brought a fiddle.

Klaus watched it all from the porch. Not as an outsider. Not anymore.

As one of them.

He had learned how to laugh again.

There was a stone at the crest of the southern hill, where the trees parted to reveal the entire valley. Klaus had placed it there himself, using stone left from the church repairs.

It bore no name.

Only the date of the fire.

And beneath it, etched in clean, precise lettering:

Truth costs. But silence rots.

He visited it once a month. Not to grieve. Not to speak.

Just to remember.

Anna wrote from San Antonio.

Twice a season.

Her letters were filled with hope. She described the hospital where she worked, the people she had helped, the woman she had become.

In one letter, she wrote:

"You showed me what it means to survive. I'm learning now how to live."

Klaus kept every letter in a box beside his bed.

One day, he would return the favor.

That fall, another newcomer arrived.

He came with a limp, a scar above his eye, and a quiet way of watching things.

Klaus spotted him by the church, then again at the smithy, then outside the orchard, leaning against a fence.

Eventually, he introduced himself.

"Name's Friedrich. From Boerne. Looking to settle. Heard this place is… honest."

Klaus said nothing for a moment.

Then nodded.

"It is now."

He invited the man for supper.

That night, they sat on the porch, watching the stars emerge one by one.

When snow dusted the valley that December, the townsfolk gathered at the church for a reading.

Liesl had written a small book—part testimony, part history, part memorial. It was called *Ashes and Orchard: The Story of Sisterdale*.

She asked Klaus to read the closing lines aloud.

He did.

His voice was clear, even as the fire snapped and cracked beside him:

"We are not who we were.
We are not yet who we must become.
But we are trying.
And sometimes, that is enough."

The church was silent after he finished.

Then came the applause.

The new year brought visitors.

A reporter from Austin. A teacher from San Marcos. A group of women from a suffrage circle in Kerrville. All curious about the "Sisterdale trial," the "fire town," the "place where they told the truth."

They found no museum, no monument, no one selling trinkets.

Only people.

Working.

Laughing.

Repairing fences, sewing, carving, planting.

And when they asked Klaus for interviews, he simply said:

"I'm not the story."

Then went back to his chiseling.

On a quiet evening in March, Klaus opened his journal—the last page.

He dipped his pen in ink and wrote:

"It has been a year since the first silence broke.
We are still here.
The wind still moves through the trees.
The truth still stings.
But it also breathes."

He closed the journal.

Wrapped it in oilcloth.

And placed it beneath a floorboard, next to a photograph, a map of Germany, and a lock of hair he hadn't touched in years.

He no longer needed them.

One night, Klaus climbed the south hill once more.

The wind was cool.

Below him, Sisterdale flickered—lamplight in windows, smoke rising from stoves, the soft hush of livestock settling down.

Peace had returned.

But not the kind Klaus had once imagined—sterile, silent, distant.

This peace was imperfect.

Hard-won.

Still tender around the edges.

But it was *real*.

As he stood beneath the stars, hands in his pockets, cedar scent thick in the air, Klaus whispered to the night:

"I'm home."

9 781088 122259